Luke threw his lightsaber into the bottom-less pit of the Death Star.

"I will never turn to the dark side," he said. "I am a Jedi. As my father was before me."

"So be it!" screamed the Emperor. "If you will not be turned, you will be killed!"

The Emperor raised his hands. Blue bolts of lightning shot from his fingers.

Luke tried to stop them, but could not. He fell to the floor, writhing in pain.

The Emperor smiled down at him. "Young fool. Now do you see the power of the dark side? Prepare to die!"

CLASSIC

STAR WARS™

Return of the Jedi™

C L A S S I C

STAR WARS™

Return of the Jedi™

Adapted by Elizabeth Levy
from the screenplay by
Lawrence Kasdan and George Lucas

Reed Books Children's Publishing

First published in Great Britain by Reed Books Children's Publishing
Michelin House, 81 Fulham Road, London SW3 6RB
and Auckland, Melbourne, Singapore and Toronto
®, TM & © 1985, 1996 Lucasfilm Ltd. (LFL).

ISBN 0 7497 2950 3

1 3 5 7 9 10 8 6 4 2

Printed and bound in Great Britain
by Cox & Wyman Ltd., Reading, Berkshire

PROLOGUE

A long time ago, in a galaxy far, far away, Rebel leaders were planning their next move against the Galactic Empire. The Rebels had fought the evil Emperor and his armies for many years. Now, for the first time, all the warships of the Rebel fleet were coming together. They would be risking everything in one giant attack.

The Rebels did not know they were doomed. The Emperor was building a new battle station, Death Star 2. Rebel Commander Luke Skywalker and his friends had destroyed Death Star 1. But Death Star 2 would be even more powerful.

CHAPTER
ONE

The two droids Artoo-Detoo and See-Threepio were far from the Death Star. They were on the hot, dusty planet of Tatooine. Luke had sent them there with a message for the gangster Jabba the Hutt.

Luke's friend Han was Jabba's prisoner. He had been carbon-frozen. Now he hung on the wall of Jabba's throne room. Luke and Princess Leia had a plan to rescue him.

Jabba's castle was dark and gloomy. The

guards were scaly green creatures. Jabba's throne room was filled with loud, ugly monsters. The ugliest was Jabba himself. He was a huge, evil blob of fat.

When Threepio saw Jabba, he shook in fear. "We're finished," he whispered. Artoo said nothing. A flap in his head opened. Then a ten-foot-tall hologram of Luke appeared.

"Greetings, Jabba," said the hologram. "I am Luke Skywalker, Jedi Knight. I am also a friend of Captain Solo. I have come to make a deal for his life. To show my goodwill, I will give you a gift: my two droids. They are hard workers."

"Oh no," gasped Threepio. "Artoo, you have played the wrong message. Master Luke wouldn't give us away."

Jabba laughed. "No Jedi Knight would make a deal. A Jedi Knight would fight.

And I will never give up my favorite piece of art." Jabba pointed to Han's frozen body. "But I'll keep Skywalker's gift."

Artoo beeped sadly. Artoo and Threepio wanted to stay together. But Jabba sent Artoo to his sail barge. He kept Threepio in his throne room. Threepio spoke more than six million languages. Jabba could use him as a translator.

The next day a strange man came to Jabba's court. The man was a bounty hunter. He had something to sell. It was Chewbacca the Wookiee, tied up in chains.

"Oh no!" cried Threepio. "Not Chewie taken too!"

The bounty hunter spoke a strange language. "Tell me what he wants," Jabba growled at Threepio.

"I'll sell you this Wookiee for fifty thousand," said the bounty hunter. Threepio told Jabba what he had said.

Jabba laughed. "Tell him I'll give him twenty-five. And his life."

The bounty hunter laughed back. "Tell that fat garbage bag he'll have to do better. Or I'll blow him up." In the bounty hunter's hand was a small silver ball. It glowed. It was a thermal detonator!

Threepio told Jabba what the bounty hunter had said. Jabba grinned. "This man is my kind of scum." He paid the bounty hunter thirty-five thousand. Then a guard threw Chewie into a cell.

Jabba gave a party for the bounty hunter. All the monsters got drunk and fell asleep.

Late that night the bounty hunter crept into the throne room.

The bounty hunter looked up at Han.

Han's face was a frozen mask. He lowered Han to the floor. Then he flipped a switch. The hard shell around Han's face began to melt. But he was very still. Was he dead?

A minute passed. Then another. Then, finally, Han's eyes opened. "I can't see!" he cried. "What's going on?"

"Shhh," warned the bounty hunter. "You're free. Soon you will be able to see again. Come, we must hurry."

"Who are you?" Han gasped.

"Someone who loves you." It was Princess Leia!

Han knew her voice. "Leia! Where are we?"

"Jabba's palace. I've got to get you out of here." Leia helped Han to his feet. He seemed weak. She held him tight. Then she and Han heard an evil laugh.

Jabba and his monsters were hiding

behind a curtain. "My, my, what a touching sight," said Jabba.

"Listen, Jabba," said Han. "I know I owe you money. I was on my way to pay you back. But…"

Jabba laughed. "It's too late, Solo. Once you were the best smuggler in the galaxy. But now you're finished. I'll decide how to kill you later."

A group of guards pulled Han away. Another guard grabbed Princess Leia. Leia saw that the guard was actually Lando Calrissian. Lando was Han's friend. Jabba didn't know this. Lando's face was hidden behind a mask.

Jabba's fat bounced with glee. "Bring the princess to me."

Lando looked worried.

Leia put her hand on his arm. "I'll be all right," she whispered.

"I'm not so sure," said Lando.

Jabba planted a slimy kiss on Leia's mouth. Then he put a chain around her neck. He kept her chained to his throne.

The guards locked Han up. Then he heard a growl from the back of the cell. A pair of strong hairy arms hugged him. Then they lifted him high off the ground. "Chewie, is that you?" shouted Han.

The giant Wookiee barked with joy. Chewie was very happy to see that Han was alive. Chewie was Han's oldest friend. He was the only co-pilot Han had ever trusted.

"What's going on around here anyway?" Han asked.

Chewie told Han that Luke was planning Han's rescue. Han felt funny. He was the one who usually did the rescuing.

Chewie barked again in his Wookiee language.

Han shook his head. "Luke, a Jedi Knight? I'll believe it when I see it."

Han gulped. He might never see again.

CHAPTER TWO

The gates of Jabba's palace opened. Luke Skywalker walked through. He carried no gun or sword. He wore the robes of a Jedi Knight.

Jabba's guards tried to stop him. Luke raised his hand. The guards began to choke. Luke entered Jabba's throne room.

"Your Jedi mind powers won't work with me, boy," said Jabba.

"Jabba, you must bring Captain Solo and

the Wookiee to me," said Luke.

Jabba's laugh was mean and hard. "Young Jedi, I shall watch *you* die."

Suddenly the floor opened. Luke fell into a pit. He heard a loud roar. A rancor jumped at him. The rancor was a giant beast. It had sharp teeth. Long arms. Terrible three-fingered claws.

Luke used his Jedi powers. He jumped high in the air. He grabbed the top of the pit. But the guards pushed him down.

Luke fell into the eye of the rancor. The monster howled. Luke ran for the door of the pit. He saw a control panel for the door. He grabbed a skull from the floor. He threw it at the panel. The panel exploded. The door fell on the rancor's head. The beast was dead.

Luke was alive. But he was not out of danger. Jabba's guards grabbed him. "You and your friends will *all* die," growled Jabba. "I will feed you to the Sarlacc."

The Sarlacc lived in a desert pit. It was a monster with tentacles. Its mouth was full of needle-sharp teeth. Hundreds and hundreds of them.

Luke, Han, and Chewie were tied up. Then they were put on a small skiff. The skiff flew across the desert on the wind. One of the guards on the skiff was Lando.

Jabba followed the skiff on his sail barge. He wanted to watch his prisoners die. Princess Leia was chained to Jabba. Artoo and Threepio were on the barge too.

Soon they came to the Sarlacc's pit. Luke was forced to walk a plank. He looked down. He could see the Sarlacc's tentacles.

"Jabba, this is your last chance!" shouted Luke. "Free us or die!"

Jabba laughed. "Throw him in!" A guard

pushed Luke off the plank. Luke used his Jedi powers. He caught the edge of the plank. He did a flip. Artoo's head opened. Luke's lightsaber was hidden in Artoo. Now it flew into his hand.

The attack was on.

Jabba screamed in anger. Leia saw her chance. She wrapped her chain around Jabba's neck. Then she jumped off the throne. She pulled the chain with all her might. Jabba died, choking. But Leia was still in chains.

Guns from Jabba's barge fired at the skiff. One blast hit Chewie. He howled in pain. Another blast sent Lando over the side. One of the Sarlacc's tentacles grabbed his leg! Lando screamed. Han reached for Lando and fell off the skiff. But his foot caught on the skiff's rail. He hung there in space. Chewie reached for Han. While he hung upside down, Han's sight came back. He could see again!

Luke had to get to Jabba's barge. He had to stop the guns. He leaped from one boat to the other. He fought Jabba's guards, but there were many of them.

Artoo rushed to Princess Leia's side. He cut her chains. "Thanks, Artoo," she said.

Leia fought her way to the barge's big guns. Then she turned them on the guards and fired.

"Good work, Leia!" shouted Luke. "Now point the guns down. That will explode the barge. Artoo and Threepio, jump!"

Threepio was afraid, but Artoo pushed him over into the sand. Luke grabbed Leia with one hand. He grabbed a rope from the barge with the other hand. Together they swung over to the skiff.

In the meantime, Han and Chewie had

pulled Lando to safety. "Sorry things got a little messy," said Luke to his friends. Just then they heard a loud *boom!* Jabba's barge exploded and caught fire.

"I've got to hand it to you, kid," said Han. "You were pretty good out there. And thanks for coming after me."

Luke grinned. "Think nothing of it."

"No, I'm thinking a lot about it," said Han. "That carbon-freeze was the closest thing to dead there is. You brought me back. And I'm grateful."

Han wasn't used to talking about his feelings. But now he wanted his friends to know how he felt. He used to be a loner. He thought he didn't need anyone else. Now he felt different.

Luke could see how much Han had changed. he was glad. Luke had risked more than his life to save Han. He had cut short his training as a Jedi Knight. Now he would return to his teacher. He would finish learning the secrets of the Force. He would become a Jedi.

CHAPTER THREE

Far across the galaxy, the Death Star hung in space. Inside the Death Star the Imperial troops stood at attention. Darth Vader was at their head. No one made a sound. The Emperor was coming.

The Emperor's shuttle arrived. First his guards came in. Their red robes were the color of blood. Then the Emperor came down the gangplank. He was a wrinkled old man, dressed in black. He walked with a cane. Under his hood his yellow eyes gleamed. They were the most frightening eyes in all the galaxy.

The Emperor stopped in front of Darth Vader, who knelt before him. "Rise, my friend. I would talk to you."

"The Death Star will be finished in time, my master," said Darth Vader in his deep voice.

"I know," said the Emperor. "You have done well. Now you wish to seek young Skywalker."

"Yes, my master."

"You need not hurry. In time he will seek you. Then you must bring him before me. He has grown strong. Only together can we turn him to the dark side of the Force." The Emperor laughed softly. "Everything is going just as I have planned. Just as I have seen."

*   *   *

Far across the galaxy, there was a little house deep in a swamp. This was the home of Yoda, the Jedi Master. Yoda had taught Luke the secrets of the Force. Yoda had always seemed ageless. Now he looked old and tired.

Luke sat in the corner of Yoda's house. His face was sad.

"Look I so bad to young eyes?" asked Yoda.

"No, Master," lied Luke. "You do not look bad."

Yoda laughed. "I do! I do! Nine hundred years old I am. When this age you reach, look as good you will not." Yoda sat on his bed. "Soon I will rest. Yes, forever sleep."

"Master Yoda, I won't let you die!" cried Luke.

Yoda smiled. "Strong with the Force you

are. But not that strong. Twilight is upon me. Soon night must fall. That is the way of things. The way of the Force."

"But I need your help," said Luke. "I want to finish my training."

"No more training do you need," said Yoda.

"Then I am a Jedi?" Luke asked slowly.

Yoda shook his head. "Not yet. Vader you must face. Only then a Jedi will you be."

A question had been burning in Luke's mind. Finally he asked it. "Master Yoda . . . is Darth Vader my father?"

Yoda took his time. "Your father he is," he finally said.

Luke gasped as if a lightsaber had cut him.

"Told you, did he?" Yoda asked.

Luke nodded.

"Sorry am I that you rushed to face him,"

sighed Yoda. "You were not ready." He shook his head and closed his eyes.

Luke felt as if he had failed. "Master Yoda, I'm sorry."

Yoda opened his eyes. "Sorry will not help. For face Vader you must. And Luke, of the Emperor beware. Great is his power. Do not think it is not. Or end up like your father you will. When gone am I, last of the Jedi will you be. Now leave me. Tell you the rest, Ben will." Yoda lay down with a deep sigh. Then his eyes closed for the last time, and he was gone.

Luke left Yoda's house. Tears filled his eyes. Artoo beeped at him. Luke passed him by. Never had he felt so alone. He put his head in his hands. "I can't do it," Luke whispered to himself. "I can't go on alone."

"Yoda and I will be with you always," said a voice. Luke's first teacher, Ben Obi-Wan

Kenobi, shimmered in front of him. Luke could feel Ben's force. But Luke was angry. He felt that Ben had lied to him.

"Ben! You told me Darth Vader killed my father!" shouted Luke. "But he *is* my father. Why didn't you tell me the truth?"

"Your father, Anakin Skywalker, turned to the dark side of the Force," said Ben. "When that happened, he took the name Darth Vader. He killed everything Anakin Skywalker believed in. He killed that good man forever. What I told you was true ...from a certain point of view."

Luke laughed bitterly. "A certain point of view!"

"Luke," said Ben softly. "Much of what we believe depends on our point of view. I don't blame you for being angry. You see, what happened to your father was my fault."

Luke looked up in surprise. How could his

father's evil ways be *Ben's* fault?

"When I first met your father," said Ben, "he was a great pilot. The Force was very strong in him. I decided to train him in the ways of the Jedi. But I was foolish. I thought I could be as good a teacher as Yoda. I was not. The Emperor turned your father to the dark side. If I had been more careful…if I had trained him better…" Ben's voice was very sad.

Luke felt his heart grow lighter. His father had not always been evil. "Then there is still good in him!" said Luke eagerly.

Ben shook his head. "No. Once I too thought Vader could be turned back to the good side. But he could not. Now he is more machine than man. Evil and twisted. And you must face him."

Luke felt pulled apart. "I can't kill my own father," he said.

"Then the Emperor has won," said Ben sadly. "And the darkness will win. You were our only hope. Yoda felt we could find and train another. Your twin sister. But now it is too late."

"My sister?" Suddenly Luke knew who Ben meant. "Leia!" he cried.

"Yes," said Ben. "When you were born, I separated you. You were raised apart, to protect you from the Emperor."

Luke wanted to cry out, "Have I learned the secrets of the Force only to use them against my father?" But he was silent.

"You cannot escape your destiny, Luke," said Ben. "You will have to face Vader again."

CHAPTER FOUR

The time for the Rebel attack on the Death Star had come. The Rebels had gathered to make their final plans. They knew that the Death Star was protected by an energy shield. The Rebels would have to destroy the shield.

But it wouldn't be easy. The shield controls were hidden—in a bunker deep in a forest. The forest was on a tiny moon called Endor. And hundreds of Imperial troops guarded Endor.

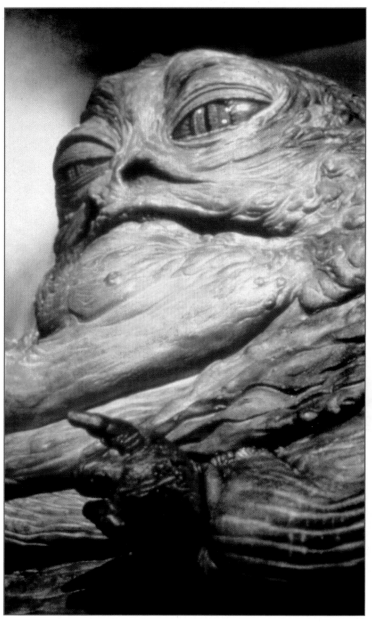

Jabba the Hutt on his throne.

Han Solo is frozen in carbonite.

Luke Skywalker comes to rescue
Princess Leia and Han.

Luke fights Jabba's guards – he has to get to the barge.

"Come on!" calls Luke as he and Princess Leia swing to safety.

A furry little face
was staring at Leia.
It was an Ewok.

Leia and Luke are
surrounded by
Imperial troops.
It's a trap.

Luke confronts his father – Darth Vader!

Admiral Ackbar leads the Rebels in
their attack.

The Emperor!

The Rebels attempt to attack the Death Star
– but the shield is still activated!

Chewbacca takes
control of an
Imperial scout
walker.

Lando zooms towards the
main reactor of the Death Star.

The Rebels and Ewoks celebrate
their victory over the Empire.

The Rebels had stolen an Imperial shuttle. They had a secret code that would help them land on Endor. Now they needed a strike team to fly the shuttle. The strike team would land on Endor. They would find the shield-control bunker and blow it up. Only then could the Rebel warships fire on the Death Star. Lando was now a Rebel general. He would lead the fleet.

Han, Leia, Chewie, and Luke would lead the Rebel strike team on Endor. They knew the danger was great. But they made a good team. They had been through a lot together.

They climbed into the stolen Imperial shuttle. Han took the pilot's seat. Chewie looked at the controls. He barked grumpily.

"Yeah, yeah, I don't think the Empire built these things with a Wookiee in mind," said Han. They blasted off into space.

As they approached Endor, Han was worried. Would their stolen code work? Luke was worried too. "I shouldn't have come," he said. "Darth Vader knows I'm here."

"Come on, kid," said Han. "You're imagining things."

But Luke was not imagining things. Darth Vader *could* feel his son coming closer. "Go to Endor and wait for him," the Emperor had told Vader. "His love for you will be his undoing." Darth Vader waited now on the tiny moon. Soon, soon, he would turn his son to the dark side.

The code worked. The Imperial shuttle passed through the shield. The Rebel strike team landed. They were in a forest of tall trees on the Moon of Endor.

Han, Luke, Leia, Chewie, and the two droids walked softly through the forest. They spotted two Imperial scouts in a clearing. Their speeder bikes were parked nearby. "Move quietly," warned Luke. "We've got to capture them. Or they'll warn the others that we're here." Before Luke could finish, Han and Chewie rushed at the scouts.

"What did you expect?" Leia asked. They knew Han was always ready for action. Suddenly Leia spotted two more Imperial scouts. She jumped on one of the speeder bikes. Luke jumped on the other one. Then they took off after the scouts.

They flew around the giant trees at 200 miles an hour. Leia made her bike fly. She caught up with one scout, but he pulled out a laser pistol. He blasted Leia's bike. She dove off and hit her head. The scout turned back to look. He hit a fallen tree. He and his bike went up in flames.

Luke caught the other scout. Then he

made his way back to Han, Chewie, and the rest of the Rebels. "Where's Leia?" Han asked.

"We got split up," said Luke. He frowned. He was afraid that Leia was hurt. "We've got to find her!"

CHAPTER
FIVE

Leia groaned. Then she blinked. A furry little face was staring down at her. It was an Ewok. Ewoks lived in the forest of Endor. Imperial stormtroopers had taught them to hate and fear people.

The Ewok held a spear. He poked at Leia with it. "Hey, cut that out," said Leia. She stood up. The Ewok backed away. "I won't hurt you. I promise." The Ewok came closer. Leia smiled. Then she patted the little Ewok on the head. The Ewok couldn't understand her words. But he decided that she was a friend. He took her to his village.

Luke and the others searched the forest for Leia. In a clearing, Chewie found a stick. Some meat was hanging from it. Chewie grabbed at it. "Wait!" shouted Luke. He sensed a trap. But he was too late. *Sproing!* Luke, Han, Chewie, and the two droids were caught in an Ewok net. Chewie howled.

"Great, Chewie!" snapped Han. "Always thinking about your stomach."

"Take it easy," said Luke. "Artoo, cut the net."

Artoo went to work with his cutting arm. In minutes they all fell to the ground. When they sat up, little Ewoks were all around them. The Ewoks chattered at them. "Threepio, can you understand what they're saying?" asked Luke.

Threepio spoke to the Ewoks in their own language. The Ewoks were amazed. They dropped their spears and fell to the ground before Threepio. "They think I'm a god!" said Threepio.

"Then order them to let us go," said Han.

"That wouldn't be proper, Captain Solo," said Threepio. "I'm not programmed to pretend I'm a god."

"Listen, you pile of bolts..." Han raised his fist at Threepio. The Ewoks didn't like the way Han was talking to their god. They tied Han, Luke, Chewie, and Artoo to long poles. They carried them to their village. But they lifted Threepio onto a throne. He traveled like a king.

When the Ewoks got to their village, they tied Han up near a bonfire. They decided to roast him for dinner.

All the Ewoks in the village came out of

their huts to watch. Leia came out with them. She was surprised to see her friends. She was even more surprised to find out what the Ewoks planned to do with Han.

"Luke, how can we stop them?" asked Leia. Han didn't like the way Leia turned to Luke for help. But there wasn't much he could do.

"Threepio," said Luke. "Tell them that you will get angry if they don't let us go. That you will use your magic."

"Master Luke, what magic?" cried Threepio.

Luke closed his eyes. He reached inside himself for the Force. Slowly Threepio and his throne rose high in to the air. Threepio began to spin. The Ewoks were frightened. They quickly untied Han and the other Rebels. Threepio was proud of himself. He had magic he didn't even know about!

That night the Ewoks and the Rebels sat together around a campfire. Threepio told the Ewoks the story of the Rebel fight against the Empire. He told them about the energy shield protecting the Death Star. And he told them why the Rebel strike team had come to Endor. "If we fail to destroy the shield," said Threepio, "the Rebel cause is doomed."

The Ewoks decided to help. They knew the forest better than anyone. They would show the Rebels the fastest way to the bunker. "Well, short help is better than no help," said Han.

CHAPTER SIX

Everyone was happy. Everyone but Luke.
He stood outside in the moonlight, alone. He
could not forget about his father.

Leia went to him. "What's wrong?" she
asked.

Luke took Leia's hand. "Leia, do you
remember your real mother? What was she
like?"

Leia was surprised by his question. "My
real mother died when I was very young,"

she said. "But she was beautiful. Gentle and kind. Why are you asking me?"

Luke turned away. "I don't remember my mother at all...and my father..." Luke couldn't speak.

"Luke, what is it?" asked Leia softly.

"Darth Vader is here now," said Luke. "On this moon."

"How do you know?" Leia was frightened. Frightened by the way Luke sounded.

"I can feel him. He has come for me. Leia, there is something I must tell you. Darth Vader is my father."

Leia grew pale. "No!" she gasped. It could not be true!

"Yes," said Luke. "And I must go to him. I must try to save him."

"Don't go, Luke! He will kill you."

"There is good in him," said Luke. "I know it."

Leia's dark eyes filled with tears. "But the Rebels need you! I need you."

"Leia, there is something else you have to know," said Luke. "The Force is strong in you. You are my sister, Leia. My twin. If I don't come back, you are the last hope for the Rebel cause."

Leia stood very still. She thought back to when she was young. And all at once she knew Luke's words were true.

Luke held her close. He knew she understood. "Good-bye, sweet Leia," he said. Then he moved down the moonlit path. He would follow his destiny.

CHAPTER SEVEN

The woods were full of Imperial storm-troopers. Luke went up to the first ones he saw. "Take me to Darth Vader," he said, handing over his weapons.

They marched Luke to a clearing in the forest. Darth Vader was waiting for him. "The Emperor told me you would come," said Darth Vader. "He believes you will turn to the dark side."

Luke stared at the heavy black mask hiding his father's face. "I know,...Father," he said.

"So you have finally accepted the truth," said Darth Vader.

"I know you were once Anakin Skywalker, my father."

Vader grew angry. "That name means nothing to me."

"It is the name of your true self," said Luke. "I know there is good in you. I can feel it."

"Ben once thought as you do," said Darth Vader. "But you do not know the power of the dark side. I must obey my master. I will take you to the Emperor. He is your master now."

With that, he led Luke away.

The next morning the Ewoks led Han, Leia, and the Rebel strike team through the forest. They reached the bunker without meeting any Imperial troops.

When they got there, Leia and Han were surprised. The bunker was guarded by just a few stormtroopers. "This will be easy," said Han.

He and Leia sneaked into the bunker. Soon they found the main control room. Leia looked up at one of the screens.

"Hurry, Han!" she cried. She could see that Lando and the Rebel fleet were in trouble out in space. They were caught—between the Death Star's shield and an Imperial Star Destroyer.

"Blast it!" said Han. "Lando's backed against a wall! Give me a second. I'll get that shield down."

"No you won't, Rebel scum," said a voice. Han and Leia spun around. Dozens of guns were pointed at them. They were surrounded by Imperial troops. Now Han and Leia understood. It had been easy to get into the bunker. *Too* easy. They had walked right into a trap!

CHAPTER
EIGHT

On the Death Star, Luke was led into the Emperor's throne room. Vader handed Luke's lightsaber to the Emperor.

"Ah, the Jedi weapon," said the Emperor to Luke. "Much like your father's. And like him, you will soon call me master."

"Never!" said Luke. "Soon I will die. And you with me."

The Emperor laughed. "Ah, you think the Rebel fleet will win. You think your friends will get to the bunker and destroy the shield. They have walked into a trap. We were waiting for them. Your fleet is lost." The Emperor cackled. He put Luke's lightsaber down near Luke.

His friends killed! Luke could not stand by and let it happen. His lightsaber flew into his hand. He swung it at the Emperor. Suddenly Darth Vader also had a lightsaber. The two blades sparked. Luke turned to fight his father.

On Endor, Imperial troops led Han and Leia out of the bunker. Now the clearing around the bunker was crowded. There were Imperial troops and Imperial walkers everywhere. It looked as if the Rebels were finished.

But up in a tree an Ewok scout was watching. He raised a horn to his lips. The

Ewoks were not going to let their new friends die. Not without a fight! The threw themselves into the attack. Suddenly rocks rained down on the stormtroopers' heads. They didn't know what had hit them.

The Ewoks were badly outnumbered. But nobody knew the forest the way they did. When the stormtoopers tried to chase the Ewoks, they got caught in Ewok traps. The Ewoks flew from the trees on homemade hang gliders. They seemed to be everywhere at once. The stormtroopers didn't know where to attack first. It was rocks against lasers. And the rocks were winning!

Soon the stormtroopers were fighting for their lives. Chewie fought side by side with the Ewoks. They captured an Imperial scout walker. Chewie took over the controls.

During the battle Han and Leia ran back into the bunker. This might be their last chance to get to the shield. Suddenly Leia heard a voice. "Hold it! One move, and you're both dead."

Han and Leia froze. Five stormtroopers had them covered. Han and Leia looked at each other. They knew that this was the end for them. But they would go down fighting.

"You know I love you," said Han.

Leia nodded.

They spun around, pulling out their laser guns. The air crackled with laser fire. When the smoke cleared, all five stormtroopers were dead. Han turned to Leia. She lay against the bunker wall, her eyes closed.

"Leia! *No!*" cried Han.

CHAPTER
NINE

Up in the throne room another battle raged. Luke was in deadly combat with his father. The last time they had fought, Darth Vader had won. But the young Jedi was stronger now. Their lightsabers flashed. Darth Vader fell. Luke raised his sword.

"Let the hate flow through you, boy!" shouted the Emperor.

Luke was winning. But he was using the dark side. He took a breath and drove his hate away. The he threw his lightsaber at his father's feet. "I do not believe you will kill me," he said.

Vader picked up Luke's sword. "You do not know the power of the dark side. It is the only way you can save your friends." Darth Vader knew that Luke loved his friends. It was his only weak spot. Luke gasped.

Vader could read his son's mind. "Leia! You love her. Obi-Wan Kenobi was wise to hide her. You say you will not turn to the dark side. But perhaps she will."

Luke could not stand to hear his father talk about Leia. His hate came flowing back. "Never!" he cried. His sword flew back into his hand. Now Luke's hate gave him a power he had never known before.

Darth Vader fell to his knees. Luke struck him. Vader's hand came apart. Luke saw that it was an artificial hand. Just like his own.

"We are so alike!" he thought.

Luke held his lightsaber at his father's throat.

The Emperor's eyes gleamed. "Good! Kill him! You will take your father's place at my side."

Darth Vader was hurt. Helpless. Luke could kill him easily. But if he did, he would lose everything. Everything Ben and Yoda had taught him.

Luke knew he had a choice. A choice he had been waiting all his life to make. He threw his lightsaber away. Into the bottom-less pit of the Death Star.

"I will never turn to the dark side," he said. "I am a Jedi. As my father was before me."

"*So be it!*" screamed the Emperor. "If you

will not be turned, you will be killed!" The Emperor raised his hand. Blue bolts of lightning shot from his fingers. Luke tried to stop them. But he could not. Darth Vader crawled to the Emperor's side.

Luke fell. The Emperor smiled down at him. "Young fool. Now do you see the power of the dark side? Prepare to die."

Bolts of lightning shot across the room. Luke's body stopped moving. He seemed dead.

Then, suddenly, Darth Vader jumped up. He grabbed the Emperor from behind. The Emperor fought back. Bolts of lightning flew everywhere. They rained down on Darth Vader's back. Vader called up the last of his strength. He carried the Emperor to the middle of the throne room. Then he threw him down into the bottomless pit.

The Emperor died. A wild wind roared

through the throne room. It pulled Darth Vader to the edge of the pit. Luke crawled to his father's side. He pulled him away from the edge. Luke fell next to his father. They were both so weak they could not move.

CHAPTER TEN

Leia was wounded. She could not move either. She had been shot in the arm. A giant Imperial walker was coming straight for her. Han threw down his gun. He would give up.

Suddenly the top of the Imperial walker opened. Chewie stuck out his head and barked. Han had never been so happy to see anyone.

Quickly he and Chewie set an explosive in

the bunker. Then they pulled Leia into the safety of the woods. *Boom!* The bunker exploded. The shield was destroyed.

Now Lando and the Rebel fleet could attack the Death Star!

The Death Star rocked under the Rebel fleet's fire. Soon it would explode.

Luke knew he had to get his father away. But the Emperor's lightning bolts had made him weak. He tried to carry his father to an Imperial shuttle. But it was no use. Luke fell.

"Go, my son. Leave me," whispered Darth Vader.

"No," Luke said. "I've got to save you."

"You already have, Luke."

Luke's eyes filled with tears. Darth Vader pulled his son close. "Luke, help me take off this mask."

"You'll die!" cried Luke.

"Nothing can stop that now. Just once, let me look at my son with my own eyes."

Gently Luke took off his father's mask. Beneath it he saw the face of an old man. A man whose eyes were full of sorrow.

"It's too late, Luke," whispered Darth Vader. Those were his last words. Darth Vader, Anakin Skywalker, Luke's father, was dead.

Luke wiped away his tears. He dragged himself to a shuttle. He had to get to Endor—and his friends.

Lando zoomed toward the main reactor of the Death Star. He fired missiles. Direct hit! Then Lando headed for Endor and safety.

The Death Star exploded in a huge ball of fire.

Luke landed his shuttle on the green

Moon of Endor. He could hear the Ewoks dancing and singing with his friends. They sounded so happy. They were free at last. They had won. Luke could not feel happy. His father was dead. Yoda was gone. He felt alone. He walked toward the Ewoks' bonfire.

Han and Leia spotted him. They ran to him and hugged him. Leia took his arm and drew him close. He was back in the circle of their warmth. And their love.

Elizabeth Levy is the author of twenty-five books for children, including *Running Out of Time* and *Running Out of Magic with Houdini*. When she is not writing or running, she likes to go to the movies or out to eat. Best of all, she likes to combine the two by eating hot buttered popcorn at the movies.

Ms. Levy says she needs to run a marathon just to make up for all the popcorn she has eaten at Star Wars movies.

She lives in New York City with her husband, who is also a Star Wars fan.